To my IMMA אִמָּא
and my MEME מֶמֶה

Inspired by a Chasidic folk tale.

At school, Shira learned all about YOM KIPPUR ‑יוֹם כִּפּוּר‑ the holiest day of the Jewish year, saying "sorry" ‑סְלִיחָה‑, looking inward, and asking, "Was I the best person I could be?"

Her teacher told the class that grownups don't eat or drink on YOM KIPPUR יוֹם כִּפּוּר. They fast צוֹם so they can concentrate on praying to God.

3

The teacher also read the story about Jonah and the big fish and the beautiful prayers we all say on YOM KIPPUR:

KOL NIDREY כָּל נִדְרִי
and NE-EELAH נְעִילָה.

Shira knew that YOM KIPPUR יוֹם כִּפּוּר is especially important and that every Jewish person should pray to God, say sorry- סְלִיחָה - and make a plan to do better the following year.

On YOM KIPPUR יוֹם כִּפּוּר Shira's parents took her to Temple בֵּית כְּנֶסֶת. They were all dressed in lovely holiday clothes, her mom and dad were holding a prayer book called a MACHZOR מַחְזוֹר, and they were each wrapped in a TALIT טַלִּית.

Shira sat next to her parents and listened to the rabbi and the cantor chanting prayers, mostly in Hebrew. She wanted very much to pray to God too, but she did not know how to read Hebrew עִבְרִית yet.

The service went on and on and Shira wanted to be part of it. She asked herself, "How can I take part in this important prayer service?"

Shira heard the SHOFAR שׁוֹפָר, so loud and powerful, "TUUUUUU" and knew what she was going to do...

9

Slowly she got up, went up
to the BIMA בִּימָה and pulled on
Rabbi Dean's TALIT טַלִּית.

10

Rabbi Dean stopped the prayer, looked down, and saw Shira next to him. He asked her, whispering, "What is it Shira?" Shira replied, "Rabbi Dean, I know I am just a little kid and I don't know much Hebrew, but I do know how important YOM KIPPUR יוֹם כִּפּוּר is and I would like to take part in this service."

Rabbi Dean looked surprised but answered, "Go ahead little Shira."

Shira stood in front of the whole congregation and said in a loud, clear voice, "I would like to offer a prayer to God! I cannot read Hebrew yet, but I can recite all of the Hebrew alphabet letters, and prayers are made from Hebrew letters! Please God, take these letters and make the most wonderful YOM KIPPUR יוֹם כִּפּוּר prayer out of them."

Shira started singing the
alphabet song she had
learned at school,

א,ב,ג,ד,ה,ו,ז,

ח,ט,י,כ,ל,מ,נ,ס,

ע,פ,צ,ק,ר,ש,ת

The whole temple was filled
with Shira's letters!

14

15

When she was finished
singing she heard people in
the temple calling, "YASHAR
KOACH!" "יִשַׁר־כֹּחַ!" and "Good
job, Shira!" and even some
clapping.

Rabbi Dean hugged Shira
and told her that her prayer
was pure and inspirational
because it came from her heart
and for sure God got it and
made the most meaningful
prayer out of her Hebrew
letters.

Shira walked back to
her seat and got hugs
and high fives from
her parents.

18

That was the last year
Shira could not read from
the MACHZOR מַחְזוֹר.
The year after she knew
more Hebrew and was able
to follow along.

חֲתִימָה טוֹבָה!

The story behind the story:

The author, Galia Sabbag, is a veteran Hebrew teacher of over fifteen years at The Davis Academy, a Reform Jewish Day School in Atlanta, GA. During her years of teaching, she has come across some beautiful, thought-provoking examples of how school affects families and their home life and how children grow in Jewish knowledge and spirituality. By witnessing these "aha" moments and/or by listening to parents' and grandparents' anecdotes, a series of stories emerged, and became lovable "Shira." She is the culmination of all Mrs. Sabbag's students throughout the years. Most of the stories in the series are real ones that actually happened to real students, interwoven with the author's creativity.

Mrs. Sabbag's stories are imbued with and enriched by Hebrew words, songs, greetings, and blessings. These stories will appeal to children in Jewish preschools, Sunday school or Jewish day schools and of course, in every Jewish home.

Coming soon in the series:
Shira in the Sukkah - a Sukkot Story
Shira and the Torah - a Simchat Torah Story
Shira and the Trees- a Tu bishvat story
and many, many more....

If you enjoyed *Shira in the Temple* you will love other stories in the Shira series: *Shabbat in the Playroom* and *RIMON for Shira*. The eBooks are available on Amazon Kindle and on Barnes and Noble Nook. Printed copies are available through the website.

Please check out the website:
www.shirasseries.com,
twitter: @shirasSeries,
or the facebook page: www.Facebook.com/Shira.series

Made in the USA
Monee, IL
31 August 2021